WHO OWNS YOU?

J. Lee Porter

Ed Teja

I0530918

Published by Nomadic Giant, LLC
www.nomadicgiant.com

Copyright 2018 by Nomadic Giant
All Rights Reserved
ISBN: 978-1-949063-02-8

"The truth is not always beautiful, nor beautiful words the truth."
— **Lao Tzu**, **Tao Te Ching**

Langley, Virginia, USA

"You want me to go undercover?" Tyler Blake looked at Ralph, his boss. He realized he was blinking stupidly, but then this had to be a joke. He wasn't a spy. "But I analyze white-collar crime."

The man nodded and it made the fat around his neck bulge out. "That makes you perfect for this assignment. You've got the financial and IT background to understand the crypto shit and that will be an important part of the program, and maybe their plans."

"But I've been working at a desk since I finished training. I'm not a field operative."

"Listen, Blake, this is the CIA, not a social club. We own your ass, and this is your assignment. You are going undercover at this anarchy conference."

"Anarchy conference? They have conferences?"

"Anarchapulco, they call it. They think they are being fucking clever because it's in Acapulco."

"But that's in Mexico. That's on foreign soil." Somehow that seemed to make it worse, more dangerous. "Don't we already have trained people there?"

"Sure. But our agent in that location has the flu.

We need to replace him."

"We have one agent there?"

He laughed. "It's fucking Acapulco, Blake. Normally it isn't exactly a hotbed of anti-government activity, but this goddamn Anarchapulco conference being held there is expected to have a couple of thousand anarchists collected there. We need eyes and ears."

"An anarchist convention? That makes no sense."

"Still, that's what's going on and the political freaks will be mixing it up with all those cryptocurrency radicals who want to destroy our economy."

Tyler sighed. Ralph was right that his background let him understand cryptocurrencies, but it probably wouldn't be a good idea to mention that he'd shifted most of his own savings into them over the last several years. They'd been his safe haven ever since he lost his ass with silver. He knew it would be pointless to explain that no one was trying to destroy anything, that it was just a matter of the old economy becoming archaic and unwieldy. He sighed. At least that part of the conference could prove interesting. "I suppose I can go, but what exactly do you expect me to do?"

"Blend in. Schmooze with the ones that seem to be ringleaders and find out if they are planning anything."

"Planning anything? Like riots? The conference is in Mexico, after all. Isn't it their problem?"

"Blake, this antigovernment shit is global. The

Mexican government isn't thrilled with these bastards either, but they need the tourist dollars and these people are rich—they're filling a major resort for a week or more. They aren't going to stop it, but they don't mind us slipping you in there to keep an eye on things."

It sounded easy enough. "No actual spycraft needed then."

"Zero. Just make some connections and keep your ears open. How hard could it be?"

# # #

When Tyler came home from work, Alice, his fiancée, was there, listening to the radio. A man was rapping out lyrics to a familiar blues tune.

"I got the keys to the Ferrari,
I'm loaded and ready to go,
I'm gonna burn out baby,
the speed limit is too fucking slow."

Tyler flinched then turned it off. Alice glared at him. "Why did you do that?"

"It's too awful. Why does that man hate Brownie McGhee so much?"

"Who?"

"That's who wrote the song."

She shrugged. "Then this guy updated it, I guess."

"Updated? He ruined it. Why can't he write his own songs to ruin?"

"He's a rap star," as if that explained it. "Why are you in such a bad mood?"

"I'm not," he said, even though he knew he was. Normally he would ignore Alice's dreadful taste in music but today he couldn't. So he told her. "I'm being sent to Mexico on assignment."

"Way cool," she said, clapping her hands.

"Really?" He told her about the assignment and being sent to Acapulco. "I'll be gone more than a week."

"Fantastic."

"I thought you'd be upset."

"About going to a resort in Acapulco? Great. We'll have a fantastic time."

"We? I'm going on what is the CIA's version of a business trip."

"We are talking Acapulco here," she said. "I'm going. Your room will be paid for. We'd just pay my airfare and food."

"I'm supposed to be working," he said.

"It's a conference. You'll be talking to people, drinking in the bar, things like that. It isn't like I'd interfere with any of that. I'd be out at the pool or in the spa."

"It's against protocol," he said. Even as he said it, he knew he was making excuses. The truth was that he didn't want her going along. "I'm supposed to be undercover. You don't take your girlfriend along when you go undercover."

"I bet you are just saying that so you don't have to take me."

Her words stung, mostly because she was right.

I didn't want to take her. "So, call Ralph and ask him if it's okay for you to go. If he agrees..."

"You ask him."

"No. I'm already on his bad side now."

"You are so much on his bad side that he's sending you to a resort in Mexico for a week." She didn't buy his argument at all.

"Exactly," Tyler said, knowing that once again he and Alice were tacitly agreeing to disagree. She wasn't going to forgive him anytime soon. Sometimes it seemed like she thought that because they were supposed to get married in a few months that she owned him. That was bothersome, but somehow not surprising. He needed to change that attitude somehow. He wanted a partner, not an owner, but how to undo what he had let happen?

"Yes, I am 100% anarchist. Anarchy, to me, is a belief that all transactions, all activity, should be voluntary. It is a peaceful philosophy of not forcing anyone to do anything and not allowing anyone else to force you to do anything."

— Jeff Berwick

Princess Mundo Imperial Hotel Acapulco, Mexico

Tyler Blake stood in the lobby outside of the main salon of the Princess Mundo International Hotel in Acapulco and laughed. "Just blend in with the crowd and see what you can learn," his boss had said. He looked at the people around him and wondered which group he was supposed to blend in with. There were men and women in business suits, looking like they'd dropped in from corporate America and others in suits who had more of an academic air about them; there were refugees from the beach in shorts and tee shirts, two women in slinky dresses and platform heels smoking cigarettes and watching the crowd looking like they'd been zapped in from a disco somewhere, and a guy wearing a rainbow-patterned sarong sort of thing that showed incredibly scrawny arms and legs. Still others dressed in an odd assortment of vendor giveaways—tee shirts with company logos, hats...

Blend in, indeed.

Tyler had chosen a middle path, wearing a short-sleeved shirt and cargo pants. He'd hoped to be inconspicuous, but no one was. As he began working the crowd, introducing himself briefly, chatting with people, he found that how he was dressed didn't seem to matter to any of them. And they were a mixed lot... farmers and entrepreneurs who had invested in cryptocurrency, business owners interested in reducing regulations, conspiracy theorists, anti-vaccine people... a strange mix of true believers of all stripes. As he looked at the literature and eavesdropped it was clear that the attendees of the Anarchapulco conference were only united in one or two ways: they resented government interference in their lives and they had come to party.

Along both sides of the hall, vendors passed out literature and talked about products. The literature was often political, primarily anti-socialist articles, which, according to this group, seemed to include a variety of US government programs; the products primarily associated with cryptocurrency in some form or another. A new crypto tied to silver competed for attention with one that promised secure communications. Another vendor sold hardware wallets.

"Hemp and Cannabidiol—CBD oil," a long-haired guy looking like he just popped in from the sixties said, pointing to literature on his table. "It's a pain reliever derived from cannabis. The government doesn't want you to know these are good for people and the environment." This guy, at least, was more what Tyler had expected.

"I can buy that legally," he pointed out.

"Sure, but the prices are jacked way the fuck up because of government regulation. People who need CBD oil can't afford it."

"You want to subsidize it?"

The man laughed. "Right. That's a government solution, dude. Just set it free." He waved his arms to indicate a bird flying.

Tyler noticed a familiar face on a man standing next to him. He turned and held out a hand. "Mike Maloney, right?" The man nodded and took his hand. "You helped me understand the danger of fiat currency way back."

"I'm glad I could be of help," he said.

"I got into silver and kept buying. Of course at $45 an ounce I took a bit of a bath."

Maloney laughed. "Who didn't? When there is market manipulation all the best theories fall apart."

"That they do."

Other people approached, taking Mike Maloney's attention and Tyler drifted about, wondering at the amazing people who were there. He saw Roger Ver, whose videos had convinced him to try cryptocurrency when silver and Bitcoin were both $23 investments, as was another precious metals advocate who was taking a closer look at cryptocurrency, David Morgan of the Morgan Report.

Inside the salon, where the speeches were being given, he found more tables, more vendors. A Canadian company mining gold in Mexico, Mexican Gold Corporation had a table across from a company using computers to mine crypto that was announcing a new facility in Iceland. Another wellness company, focused on the things the governments were doing to the water supply, sold filtration systems and passed out information on the dangers of fluoride.

Some of this seemed rather out there to Tyler, yet it was harmless and Ralph had made it clear that he wasn't there to learn about the harmless. He wanted the scoop on conspiracies and frauds.

"International fraud, most of it digital is growing, Tyler," his boss had said. "This conference is putting the political crazies in touch with the guys who are pushing technology in ways we can't control it. I want to know what they are talking about and who is doing the loudest talking."

"Doesn't the agency already monitor all these people?" he asked.

"Shit yes. And the chatter is all over the place. But you have a finance and tech background—enough to pick up on the threads of things and see where they lead. You need to identify the code words, the key concepts we need to scan for."

And so, here Tyler was, staying in a five-star resort on the taxpayers' dime, trying to filter through the chaos of complaints about government intervention. The irony wasn't lost on him that without the anarchists, he'd be at home, dealing with snow in wintry Virginia.

The tricky part of his job certainly wasn't finding suspicious conversations. Hell, the 'plots,' as his boss at Langley saw them, were all over the place. All you had to do to get involved in discussions of political intrigue was to say hello in a bar. The problem was... most of the schemes he overheard or was told outright were not, in any way, shape or form, illegal. For some of the things that were emerging, such as the myriad applications of tokens and blockchain, there weren't any laws concerning them at all. The people at the IRS might see them as ways to avoid taxes, but even they hadn't agreed on a clear definition of what cryptocurrency was—securities, real property, or money. So, there wasn't much to report.

Besides, Ralph was mostly concerned with the political, the radicals who wanted to be able to travel without passports, or other nefarious things. Yet, as he sat in on lectures, as he drank with people in the bar during breaks, he began to realize that almost without exception the 'anarchists' he was meeting weren't plotting anything. They were individually and, at times collectively, seeking out ways to be left alone. Some of the methods might be sketchy, or even marginally legal, but there was no insurrection intended.

"Blockchain frees us from the central control of the government," the communications people told him. While Ralph and his superiors would fear that, and certainly hate it, it was hardly a revolution.

More of a sidestep around things, like dropping out and moving to Tahiti without telling anyone.

Tyler found himself liking these people. Well, some were crazies of course, but harmless enough. Many were good business people trying to make money—and they seemed to be doing that. And the vendors were like vendors anywhere. They had a product that they thought suited whatever the hell demographic this was.

One vendor, in particular, caught his attention. Two attractive women were running a booth wearing black tee shirts that said "DateChain" on them. It was, he learned a startup.

"We are having our initial coin offering in a couple of months," a dark-haired lady told him. She had a name tag that said 'Tara' and appeared to be in her late twenties or early thirties.

"Coin offering?"

"We are using blockchain to provide a secure escort service," she said, sounding very matter-of-fact.

"Escort service?" That caught him off guard.

She nodded. "Worldwide."

"But that's illegal," he said.

She laughed. "You must be American. In many places it's a perfectly legal activity," she said with a smile. "In others, only solicitation is illegal, not prostitution."

"But your website..."

"We aren't located in any country. We are in the blockchain."

"But you have to based somewhere."

"Sure. But there are countries where both prostitution and cryptocurrency are recognized and permitted. That's where our servers are, so that's where we are."

Tyler scratched his head. "But..."

She handed him a brochure. "Go to the investor's website and read up. Think about the company and come back with any questions." She handed him a business card. "Tara Hutchins, President, DateChain."

Tyler looked at her. "It's your company?"

"Partly. I'm a founder and president."

"That's surprising," he said.

"Why? It shouldn't be. Escorts have to be business people."

That made a lot of sense. "But a company is rather visible, isn't it. I thought you'd want to stay below the radar." Radar, meaning people like him who were paid to notice.

She shrugged. "We are changing things. Asserting our rights."

"Your rights?"

"The right to ownership of our bodies and lives. Why should a government have the right to say what a free individual does with her own body? They let people get in a ring an bash each other's brains out on pay-per-view; people can screw their brains out and it's fine, but if a woman or a man wants to be paid for providing their body to give another human sexual pleasure some governments think they have the right to prevent that—to make it against the law. It's the majority enslaving the minority."

"So it's a political statement?"

"It's a business, but there is inherently a political implication to almost every business. In this case, it's the idea that people own themselves. Our company helps escorts work safely. We are doing this for ourselves."

"We?"

She smiled. "I'm an escort," she said.

For reasons he didn't understand, her answer stunned him.

# # #

Back in his room, Tyler Blake took Tara's advice. He was an analyst and she'd given him a lot to analyze. He opened his laptop to research her initial coin offering but before he could go to the website, he saw that he had an email from his boss.

"Find anything to report?" it asked.

He hit reply. "I've met a bunch of people who don't like to be regulated in any way, and some very new age people saving the world with yoga. Not much else." Then he hit reply. He knew that would inspire a tart response telling him to dig deeper for his country, but that was okay. He could ignore it.

There was also an email from Alice but he wasn't in a mood to read it. Maybe he'd check it out later.

He went to the DateChain website and started reading. He hadn't paid a lot of attention to ICOs in general. In fact he realized that he didn't know anything about them. He needed someone to help him understand why they were happening, popping up across the financial landscape like wildflowers. Certainly they were tied in with the companies using blockchain to do business, but a coin offering wasn't essential to doing that.

Given that the resort was lousy with garrulous experts, Tyler went downstairs to find one. He went into the Starbucks and got a coffee and took it outside to the breezeway, where there were chairs and tables where small groups of people were talking while they enjoyed their coffee and pastries or sandwiches. He recognized a young guy he'd seen at the booth for one of the wellness companies that was somehow involved with blockchains. As he walked over to the table, the man smiled up at him and pointed to an empty chair. "How's it going?"

"I'm getting a little confused by all the terminology," Tyler told him as he sat, thankful that the man saved him the trouble of prying. "Your company, for instance... you are going to have an ICO, and initial coin offering."

"That's right."

"Why not an IPO? They are well understood by investors."

The man smiled. "Because when you have an IPO you hold it in a country and immediately become tied up with all their rules and regulations about securities. With an ICO we are free of that. And why would a company making tee shirts in Guatemala and selling them in Ecuador want to get burdened with that, or with US taxes, if you follow your logic and go where the investors are."

"Okay, I can see that. Tax and regulation avoidance."

The man grinned. "Besides, who makes money in an IPO? Mostly it goes to the lawyers and the bank that underwrites it. And small investors are cut out of the action."

"The idea is to protect everyone involved," Tyler said.

The man laughed. "So the same government that doesn't care if you lose half your paycheck in taxes and gamble the rest away in Vegas feels the need to protect you from getting into the early stage of an investment that your instincts tell you is a great opportunity?"

Tyler laughed. "That's not the intention, I suspect."

"At best, all that does is protect the poor while allowing the rich the first shot at real money making opportunities. Protecting people from risk, protects them from the rewards too. So, in our case, we think average people will see value in our company, and that value can be greater without government interference. The only I way I know of to allow investment and still be free is through an ICO. And as a bonus, with companies like ours, you are protected from the failure of a fiat currency."

"A small investor can buy silver or gold," Tyler pointed out. They offer protection."

"Only if the government doesn't confiscate it."

"Why would they do that?"

"The reason isn't important, not as important as

the fact that they've done that before."

"When?"

"In 1933. Executive Order 6102. Franklin D. Roosevelt decided that hoarding precious metals was making the recession worse. That was all it took. He implemented it under the Trading with the Enemy Act of 1917. So, thinking they wouldn't do it is foolish. A better play is to invest in mining companies outside the US. There are some here, and some that are truly decentralized. Even if the effort to suppress this became global, if they want to try confiscating a real decentralized cryptocurrency, best of luck to them. If they go after the owners, well, it would be like trying to arrest smoke."

As he thought over what the man said, Tyler's cell phone beeped. He glanced at it and saw an Inclement Weather Alert. "Massive snowstorm blankets Virginia." He swiped it away and saw the home page with a picture of the sun, and the notation that it was 78 degrees in Acapulco.

"Problem?" the man asked.

"Just cold weather hitting Virginia hard and making me glad I'm here."

"Wow, Virginia. Home of the CIA." Tyler flinched. "Makes me wonder," the man said... "a conference like this going on... how many Feds you think they've sent to keep track of us?"

Suddenly Tyler tensed. "What makes you think they've sent Feds here?"

"They always hate what they don't control," the man said. "I mean, think about the fact that what we are doing isn't legal or illegal. It's something new, something they don't understand. Like I said, they'll have their hands full trying to stop cryptocurrency and business based on blockchain from taking over. They have to know that. So my guess is that the people who still pay taxes are funding a bunch of black shoes to come here for fun in the sun—and there is nothing useful they can learn."

Tyler was wearing sandals and still had to resist looking at his own feet. "Well, they do collect data."

"And sit around with us, people here on our own dime trying to do business, or understand the nuances and developments. The way you are. They send spies to listen to people having honest discussions and taxpayers, who can't afford to stay here, pay for it all."

The truth struck home and made Tyler uncomfortable. The man was sharing information openly. Everyone here was. He finished his coffee. "Well, thanks for the education. I didn't think about a lot of those things before."

The man handed him a card. "The investor information is on the web site if you decide it might be safer with us than in fiat currency."

Tyler put it in his pocket. "Well, I will definitely take that under advisement."

With new insights spinning about in his head, Tyler went back to his room and returned to the DateChain website. He read with his usual thoroughness and was impressed. The incredibly businesslike discussion of what he had always thought of as part of the dark underbelly of commerce struck him as incongruous if not just plain weird. Although it mentioned escorts providing services for their clients, it left the details to the imagination of the reader. The discussion was of how the platform would act as a broker, a go-between that ensured good customer service, a quality experience. Clients had to create a profile and could pay in cryptocurrency or cash. The service provided a date book, much like the one in the major dating services, where a client could learn about prospective escorts in the area.

The most remarkable page, to Tyler, was the one written to explain to escorts how to sign up and use the service. They had to prove they were over nineteen to ensure there was no sex trafficking. Then they created a profile and could list specialties. They'd be able to see ratings of clients provided by other escorts and there were multiple levels of screenings of the clients they could choose from.

The key word that he kept coming back to was 'choice.' The lectures on libertarianism were naturally about freedom of choice, and now he began to see why Tara and her company were here at this conference. He had begun to see that the appeal would be to investors looking for both innovation and a chance to work in the shadows. This business proposal had a definite political dimension to it—the company fully intended to work around the laws of individual nations.

The way they were going about it was clever.

Clearly the same approach would work for so many things where crime was relative—the idea that something illegal was a national, regional or even local proposition, not something like murder that could be universally frowned on. With so many places legalizing marijuana and the network of global tax deals so complex, this was fertile ground. This, Tyler was certain, was what unnerved the authorities and was exactly the sort of thing that his own boss wanted to hear about.

The trick was that the company, it's formation, was perfectly legal and unless they carried out business where it was illegal, there wasn't much a government could do about it; even then they could only prosecute the illegal activities in their own area.

Clearly the women who were signing up were treating their work as a business. And the ones already on the site, the examples, were beautiful.

The next day by the time he reached her table in the conference room, Tyler had several questions buzzing in his head. "You've done such a thorough job of researching and planning...why not use this model for a business that doesn't run afoul of local laws?" he asked.

Tara laughed. "Name a business that doesn't run afoul of local laws and regulations. Most just consider it a cost of doing business. Think of the legal battles Amazon and Google fight in Europe and China. We prefer to be more off the radar and decentralized. That way no government can demand we defend what we are doing, which is simply marketing something we own."

"And the escorts that join your service all feel that way?"

"I wouldn't know," she said. "I imagine some of them just see us as a way to reach the right clientele and, not incidentally, keep a larger portion of the fee she negotiates. We take a transaction fee, not the huge cut a pimp or escort service demands. Each person will have her own reasons, her own philosophy. We don't care what that is as long as they adhere to our standards and our business practices."

"I'm trying to understand," he said.

The room was quiet for the moment. Tara turned to the other woman, Eileen. "I'm taking a break." The woman nodded. "Let's go get a coffee," she told Tyler.

The offer surprised him, but then he found himself constantly being surprised in this crowd. He'd expected that he'd be treated as an outsider, that no one would talk to him seriously until he'd somehow proven himself. That was the way covert groups operated. Instead, it was more common to have some business type walk up, offer him a beer, and shout, "Hey, fuck the government, right?"

It had his head swimming.

He followed Tara to an outdoor buffet restaurant where they took a table in the sun and ordered coffee. Nervous blackbirds were dancing around, lurking on the umbrellas of nearby tables and making forays to attack unprotected plates and returning with bits of bread, fruit, or pastries. They looked well fed.

"Why are you here, at this conference?" she asked him.

The question surprised him and his body tensed. Was she onto him? Had his naive questioning blown his cover? "To learn," he said. "I've heard so much about this movement."

She laughed. "There's no movement."

"No? You get fifteen hundred people to go to Mexico to talk politics and technology and there's no agenda."

She shrugged and put sweetener in her coffee. He watched her long fingers holding the spoon as she stirred it. Something about the image transfixed him and it took a few moments to realize that he was trying to reconcile the idea that this woman he was chatting with was an escort and an entrepreneur. Actually, he was trying to reconcile his preconceptions of both. He didn't know any entrepreneurs, and he doubted he knew any escorts. He'd never hired one.

"Are the people who go to computer shows a movement?" she asked. "Are people who share an idea necessarily a movement? It doesn't seem inherent to holding a convention. I'm here because these people are more likely to support my company than investors at large, and a good number of the attendees are filthy rich. Other people are here for much the same reason. If you want to learn about the principles or theories the people espouse you'd do better to stay home and read their books and watch their videos. They are glad to tell anyone who will listen what they stand for, and why."

She sat back and tasted the coffee. "Should've walked over to the Starbucks next to the main lobby," she said. "This is weak."

Tyler looked at her, wondering. She made it sound so simple. "Okay, forget the others and political agendas for the moment," he said. Hearing himself talking he realized how far he was getting from the mission he'd been sent to accomplish. Tara and her company might eventually get entangled with law enforcement, and perhaps criminals were involved with the operation, but he was looking for networks of radicals, operatives. This was just his own curiosity.

"There is a theme to most people's motives for coming here," she said. "Including mine. I'm doing what it takes to free myself and the other escorts from the control of pimps, criminal organizations, in which I include governments." She pointed to herself. "This is my body. Like I told you before, it isn't right that they have a damn thing to say about how I use it. If I want to monetize sex, sell my body, that's between me and my client. My company makes it possible to do that more safely and without bribing cops or other crooks."

"If I didn't know better I'd say you were a tad cynical about cops."

"They've not done much to make my life easier, Tyler. They tend to think they own other people, just as other people in authority do. Not all of them, but enough. It's the way they are taught."

He turned the conversation back to her business, still curious. The more Tyler learned, the more the business model intrigued him.

She laughed. "You are either deciding whether or not to invest or thinking of applying for a job."

He joined her laughter. "It probably sounds like that."

"Well, if it's your thing, and your questions about financial matters make me think it might be, I want you to know that we need a new chief financial officer for DateChain. The woman acting as our CFO at the moment is part-time. She has a full-time gig at an investment bank. That's worked well up to now, but at this point in our roadmap the investors want to see a real staff. If you think you are looking for a new opportunity and a challenge, send me your resume. As you can imagine, we will have a challenging few years ahead of us."

Two things about that statement shocked Tyler. The first was that someone that high up in the financial food chain had been working with Tara's company, even just helping out. The second was that he found himself actually considering it for a moment, picturing himself pulling this company together, financially. What a challenge that would be, and his experience with international monetary systems, studying the ins and outs of financial transfers, made him an ideal candidate.

And Tara was serious. She was staring at him, waiting for a reply.

"I..." before he got the words out, he was assaulted by a huge splat of bird shit that landed on the leg of his shorts. "Damn," he said, grabbing a napkin and wiping at it, mostly spreading it around. "I'm going to have to go change clothes."

Tara was laughing. "That was priceless," she said. "Listen, I'm leaving in an hour. We've already checked out and need to get back and sort out some things." She stood and put a hand on his. It sat there, light, warm, sending a tingle through him. "Filling that job is important, so if you think you might be right for it and are interested, get in touch. If you know someone else good, have them contact me."

Then she left. Tyler put the charge on his room bill, amused at the idea of the CIA paying for her coffee, then he went to his room and changed.

When he rejoined the conference it was with more questions than ever, and few, if any, had to do with uncovering terrorist attacks or assaults on the republic that was The United States of America.

At the break, he saw Jeff Berwick, the founder of The Dollar Vigilante, the conference organizers. He walked up to him and shook his hand. "I'm new to this, Mr. Berwick, but it's an impressive conference."

"It is," Berwick said, obviously pleased. "It's growing like crazy. I never imagined it this big and next year it will be bigger."

# # #

On the flight back to Virginia, Tyler found himself digesting everything he'd seen and heard. He would have to make a detailed report, and the powers that be would be unhappy that he hadn't uncovered some group planning an armed revolt, so they'd question him.

And when it was over, they'd send him back to reviewing stock trades, spreadsheets, and bank transfers, looking for the evidence of money being used to finance terrorist cells. He sat back in the seat, looking out at puffy white clouds in a clear, blue sky and, for the first time, thought about the people the records belonged to. He was making a career out of snooping into what were largely legitimate transactions, the financial records of people who had done nothing wrong. There was no 'presumed innocence' in his office. Everything was suspicious until proven otherwise.

His plane landed on time, and during the taxi ride from the airport, he thought of the people he'd met. They'd been a cross-section of people, from all walks of life, who were attempting to assert their right to be free. Through political action, through taking charge of their own financial future, through eating right and paying attention to wellness, they were taking ownership of their lives.

And he was the enemy—of their independence, of their financial security, of their freedom to live without scrutiny.

Langley, Virginia, USA

When he got home he found Alice waiting for him. Her expression told him that his welcome would be exactly what he had expected, had feared. She'd been mad when he left, and her anger at being left behind hadn't abated. It didn't help that he'd ignored her messages. In the context of that conference, he couldn't bring himself to deal with them, with her issues. Too many new ideas had been exploding in his head to deal with old baggage.

"I hope you are intending to take me out to dinner," she said. "You owe me."

"Why is that?" he asked. For once, her forceful assertion didn't upset him. He found it odd and illogical. "Assuming I had a grand time in Mexico while you dealt with a snowstorm, why does that mean I owe you anything?"

"Because..." She wasn't able to finish the thought. Finally an idea came to her. "Because I'm your fiancée."

"I'll take you out," he told her, "because I want to eat out and so do you. I don't accept that I owe you a dinner or anything else."

She was silent, but something in her eyes told him she wasn't satisfied with his attitude. At some point, the relationship with her had gone terribly wrong; only now did he begin to understand what it was. "You're mad at me," he said.

"Hurt and upset. Not mad. You don't act like you love me."

"Doing what someone tells you to because you are afraid of upsetting them isn't love. Demanding that another person think only of your happiness, even when it costs them their own, isn't an act of love either."

"You went off without me."

"Yes, I did."

Her look changed to confusion and he knew she was wounded. He didn't want to deliberately hurt her feelings, but he no longer was going to let her dictate how he felt and what he did. And, if she was hurt, at least it kept her quiet that night.

When they got back to the apartment that night she came onto him, using the sex card. Because the idea pleased him, he made love to her but found it remarkably unsatisfactory.

His entire existence with Alice was unsatisfactory and he saw that it was nothing he'd ever sought; he'd just let it happen, let it evolve. That had to change.

The next morning he learned that his boss Ralph was as disappointed in him as Alice. "You brought me shit," he said. "There isn't anything actionable in any of it."

"Was I supposed to make something up? None of the people I talked to or overheard wanted to do anything to damage the US government. The most they wanted was to find ways to withdraw from its control, to assert their ownership of their own lives."

"And how is a republic supposed to function if everyone does that? That undermines the system."

"The point is, not playing the game isn't illegal. If someone goes to Amsterdam and smokes pot, it isn't illegal."

Ralph's face grew red. "Damn it, you know what I mean."

Tyler looked at him. "Actually, Ralph, I don't think I do. In fact, I'm not sure you know what you mean. I get that you are frustrated that these people aren't doing anything illegal to accomplish a goal you are against, but I don't see what we are supposed to do about that."

"We aren't cops, Tyler. We don't enforce the laws. Sometimes we break them to keep this country safe."

The idea startled him. "Really? Then who are we keeping it safe for? The people you want me to find things on are citizens too. If we have a democracy and they all voted to abolish the government then from a legal point of view, that's the will of the people and we'd be out of work."

"That's just hyperbolic political rhetoric," Ralph said. "They just want to run things."

"You mean like the Democrats and Republicans?"

"Don't be a wise-ass, Blake. Your career is on thin ice as it is. Go write a full report and give me something I can use or you will be counting paper clips for the next 20 years if you have a job at all."

Back at his desk, Tyler took out his notes and read them over. There were things he could take out of context that would please his boss, but as he read over them, he pictured the people who were talking, remembered who and what they were. Ralph wanted him to construct a context that would allow them to be investigated. That had to change too.

He switched on his computer and typed: "Report on Anarchapulco 2018. Met some fascinating people. Had a good time. Drank too much. Ron Paul's speech was pretty cool and probably rather subversive, although everything he said is in his books already. The resort was lovely, but overpriced and the trip was a waste of taxpayer money."

At the bottom, he typed: "P.S. I quit."

He picked up his personal phone and dialed a number he'd memorized. "Hello, Tara, it's Tyler Blake... from the conference."

"Well, well. That was quick." She sounded happy to hear from him.

"I just sent you my resume. I'd like to talk about the CFO job you mentioned."

"I'm actually reading it now, Tyler. Very, interesting background. Given your current employment, now I understand why you were interested in movements that might be meeting in Mexico."

"And I learned there weren't any."

"No? You seemed to feel differently in Mexico."

"There weren't any of the kind I was sent to find. None worth mentioning in my report. As a result of that report, I need to warn you that my current employer isn't likely to give me a recommendation. And I just quit."

She laughed. "They didn't like what you learned."

"Not in the least. They expected certain results and I didn't come through."

"Well, I'm not likely to call human resources at Langley for a reference. But what happens if I don't hire you? I feel like I've led you on."

"Not at all. If this doesn't work out then I'll have to take my freedom elsewhere. There are tons of startups. None as interesting to me as yours."

"What makes my company so attractive?"

"I think that the legal and personal freedom aspects will make for an amazing challenge that would be fun to tackle."

"Fun?"

"Yes. I've decided to start having fun."

"Good for you. So, are you ready to travel? Starting now? We need to set up some business centers in Europe."

He thought about Alice for a few, long seconds. He thought about the things in his apartment... his possessions. They meant nothing. "I'm ready. I don't have anything keeping me here."

"And you can help secure our records?"

"My current employment has given me a reasonable amount of experience in keeping financial and any other records away from prying eyes."

"You know the pay will be small to start. We are putting the money in the business."

"The pay isn't important. I'm counting on

getting tokens and I'm pretty sure they are going to be worth a bundle very quickly."

There was a pause. "Are you sure you want to be a major player in a business that is actively looking for the shadowy areas of international law? You do understand that, right?"

"I've given it a lot of thought and yes."

"Then you are hired." The sigh of relief that escaped his lips surprised him. "I'll send you an e-ticket and we will meet in London in two days. We have an investor meeting there."

"Fantastic."

"And congratulations."

"Thanks. I'll do a great job."

"Oh, I know that. You'll work your ass off for us. I meant congratulations on deciding you have the right to own yourself."

A sudden rush of happiness ran through him. "Thank. It feels fantastic," he said.

"Then I'll see you in London."

As he hung up, Ralph stormed into his office waving a printout. It was the report he'd filed. "What the fuck is this, Blake? What the hell is going on? Is this some kind of joke."

"You always said the agency owned me, Ralph. I just reclaimed the title to my life. Now I own myself... for better or worse."

"What the hell do you mean?"

"It's all about freedom, Ralph."

"And you were sent to protect America's freedom."

"Real freedom is all about ownership, Ralph.

Think about it. Who owns you? If the government or the agency owns you, you aren't really free."

"You were infected by those fucking communists."

"Communists don't like free individuals, Ralph. Neither does the agency, so I'm quitting."

"You will regret this. There will be a black mark on your record."

Tyler doubted it very much. "Maybe I will, Ralph. But if I do, at least I'll regret making my own mistakes, not that of a faceless agency." He took out his ID and slid it across the desk. "You'll want these."

"You're quitting right now? Today?"

"There's no time like the present." He stood, feeling oddly lightheaded. The feeling would pass, of course. Reality would descend on him to remind him that he hadn't solved all of his problems, that maybe he had made his life harder, but that was all right. It was his hard life—he'd own it for good or evil.

The first task was to face Alice and tell her the truth. He needed to tell her that she didn't own him, that he didn't recognize her claim on him. He would tell her that he was packing to leave forever. However that went down, he was going to London, to his future. He wanted to take a look at the company's organization and its books so he could see how things needed to be structured... He was thinking of ways to do international business via blockchain and keep the organization off the radar—all radars except that of investors, clients, and escorts.

There was so much to do, and every bit of it exciting when you knew who owned you.

# # #

Also by the authors

<u>CRYPTO SHRUGGED</u>

Bitpats Book 1

When Ayn Rand released <u>ATLAS SHRUGGED</u> in 1957 the world was at a tipping point. The disruptive force of the industrial revolution had driven technology and social changes at an incredible pace that overwhelmed the traditions and mores of the Western world. Her book looked at the polarization between the creators and the parasites, the ones who developed and used the technology for what they perceived as good, and the ones who used it for control, to obtain increasing power.

The book solved nothing, but it did provide insights into possibilities and hopes, as well as an unfortunately prescient look at the future. Today, in 2018, new disruptive forces are at work and once again overwhelming the world in both cultural and economic ways. The internet, and in particular the internet of money—blockchains and cryptocurrencies are precipitating a mad scramble for control. The decentralizing effect of the technology unnerves the powers that be and they strive to control it. Other forces want to use it for their own goals, ranging from the beneficial to malignant.

The players in Ayn Rand's time were industrialists, politicians, bureaucrats, philosophers, and pirates. Exchange programmers for the industrialists, libertarians for pure philosophers (and some of the pirates) and the cast remains much the same.

This, then is the canvas we have drawn for <u>CRYPTO SHRUGGE</u>D. Atlas has long ago disappeared and our world is held aloft by less tangible forces, yet there is still the possibility that amid the chaotic struggle for dominance, they too will shrug. And what happens then?

To see all of the books and stories, go to

www.nomadicgiant.com

About the Authors

J. LEE PORTER

J. Lee Porter is a former IT specialist, programmer and data analyst for banking, security, and government agencies. He left the IT world behind on July 4th, 2016, declaring it his personal independence day to travel the world full time in search of inspiration for his writing.

J. Lee Porter on Amazon www.amazon.com/J.-Lee-Porter/e/B079DGS7HF/
@JLPorterAuthor on Twitter

ED TEJA

Ed Teja is a writer a poet, a musician and boat bum. He writes about the places he knows, and the people who live in the margins of the world. After being friends with tech giants, pirates, fisherman, and a coterie of strange people for many years, he finds the world an amazing place filled with intriguing, if sometimes crazed characters.

Ed Teja on Amazon www.amazon.com/Ed-Teja/e/B001K8HYZU
@ETeja on Twitter